THE SEVEN AND THE LION HUNT

Enjoy another thrilling adventure with the
Secret Seven. They are Peter, Janet, Pam,
Colin, George, Jack, Barbara and, of
course, Scamper the spaniel.

When Brutus the lion escapes from the
Jungle Circus the Secret Seven decide to
help out. They know all the local hiding
places, and Scamper the spaniel is very
good at tracking, but can the Secret Seven
succeed in capturing a real lion?

D0552562

The Seven and the Lion Hunt

A new adventure of the
characters created by
Enid Blyton, told by Evelyne
Lallemand, translated by
Anthea Bell

Illustrated by Maureen Bradley

KNIGHT BOOKS
Hodder and Stoughton

British Library C.I.P.

Lallemand, Evelyne
    The seven and the lion hunt.
    I. Title   II. Les sept à la chasse au
    lion. *English*
    843'.914[J]   PZ7

ISBN 0 340 32888 6

Printed and bound in Great Britain for Hodder and Stoughton Paperbacks, a division of Hodder and Stoughton Ltd., Mill Road, Dunton Green, Sevenoaks, Kent TN13 2YA. (Editorial Office: 47 Bedford Square, London WC1B 3DP) by Cox & Wyman Ltd., Reading.

CONTENTS

Chapter One

THE CIRCUS IS COMING

It took Peter no time at all to get home from school when he had a fat, shiny conker to kick down the road ahead of him! He had found a really beautiful conker in the playground, and now he was on his way home with his satchel on his back, running, passing and shooting with his find as if it were a football. As he chased along he dreamed of being in one of the top First Division football teams . . . but his daydream soon came to an end when he shot at an imaginary goal, and the conker disappeared underneath the double doors of somebody's garage. Peter lay down on his tummy and tried to reach under the doors, but he couldn't find his lovely conker. Well, never mind, he could always get another one in the playground tomorrow. There were plenty on the big horse chestnut tree.

As he got up again, he was surprised to find himself facing the picture of a huge lion's head! He had been so absorbed in his game with the conker that he had never noticed the poster advertising a circus which was stuck to the garage doors. It showed a magnificent lion with fiery eyes and a huge mane, his mouth open to show long, sharp teeth.

Peter read the big red and gold letters on the advertisement. They said JUNGLE CIRCUS, and there was a sticker on the top right-hand corner, to say the circus would be giving three performances in the village, on Thursday evening and on Sunday afternoon and evening.

Well, thought Peter, this would be a good moment for a meeting of the Secret Seven. Since he was head of the Society, it was up to him to let all the other members know. So he hurried home to Old Mill

House, thinking that as this was Monday evening, the Seven hadn't got very long to decide if they were going to see one of the performances given by the Jungle Circus.

Scamper the golden spaniel met Peter at the door of the farmhouse, as usual – and wouldn't let his young master go in until Peter had made a great fuss of him!

'Scamper, the Secret Seven will soon be calling a very special secret meeting!' Peter told him quietly. 'And you can stand on guard for us again!'

Peter's mother interrupted this conversation. She was in the kitchen, and she called out to him.

'Gracious, you're home early today, Peter! Tea's not ready yet, but you can cut a slice of bread if you like, and there's plenty of milk!'

Peter didn't like to tell his mother the only reason he was home so soon was because he'd been playing football with a conker all the way. It didn't sound a very dignified thing for the head of a secret society to do! He made himself two jam sandwiches and drank a big mug of milk. Then, before going up to his own room to do his homework, he asked his mother if he could use the telephone to ring up his friend Jack.

'Yes, all right,' she said. 'Just so long as your telephone call doesn't last three-quarters of an hour, like the last one you made!'

Peter went into the sitting room, taking care to close all the doors after him, because everything to do with the Secret Seven had to *be* secret! Then he sat

9

down in an armchair and picked up the receiver. He knew Jack's number off by heart, so he soon got through.

'Hallo, Jack!'

'Hallo – is that you, Peter?' said a voice. Coming over the telephone line, it didn't *sound* much like Jack, but it *was* him!

'Jack, have you seen that advertisement?' asked Peter.

'Advertisement? What advertisement?'

'Didn't you know? There's a circus coming here – it sounds really exciting.'

'Oh, wait – hold on a minute!' said Jack at the other end of the phone.

Peter heard a confused sort of noise over the line. He was wondering what on earth his friend could be doing when Jack spoke again.

'Sorry, Peter – I had to go and look out of the window! Can you hear it? Listen!'

Peter could just make out the faint sound of music and voices.

'It's the circus van!' Jack explained. 'It's just going down the road, and there are great big posters stuck to it. There's a loudspeaker too, announcing three special performances here on Thursday evening and on Sunday — '

'Afternoon and evening!' Peter told him, interrupting. 'Yes, that's exactly why I rang you up. How about all of us going – the whole Secret Seven?'

'Good idea!' said Jack. 'What's more, it's quite a

long time since we held a meeting and did something exciting together.'

Later that afternoon, when he had done his homework, Peter knocked on the door of his sister Janet's room. He found her sticking stamps into her big stamp album, the one with the red cover.

'Janet,' he said, 'the Secret Seven are going to have a meeting.'

'Oh good!' said Janet. 'Will we have an adventure too?'

'Well – I don't know about that, but just now I want you to find that fine new fountain pen of yours, and I'll dictate a letter telling everyone to come to the meeting.'

Peter decided to call the meeting for Wednesday at eleven o'clock. There wouldn't be any school that day, because the school boiler needed overhauling, so all the children had the day off. What luck! And Peter also suggested that before they met each of the Secret Seven ought to try finding out something about the Jungle Circus, because having a circus in the village was certainly the most exciting thing to happen to them for some time.

So ever since nine o'clock that Wednesday morning, the Seven had been wandering round the field where the circus folks were camping. To look at the children, you'd never have thought they were a well-organized secret society. But they were really all busy finding out what they could about the circus, the

11

people who worked there, and how they lived.

Peter and Jack were watching three men driving big stakes into the ground with mallets. Colin was lending a hand to two boys who were unfolding the canvas of the Big Top itself. Sitting on the steps of a caravan, Janet and Barbara were talking to a fair-haired little girl. As for George, he was walking round the animal cages, a purse tightly clutched in his hand. At last Pam arrived, out of breath, half an hour after all the others. She started going round the caravans, and soon saw a fat, cheerful-looking woman cooking a big pan of chips.

The Seven had two hours before their meeting in the shed in Peter and Janet's garden, which was their headquarters, and they were spending that time getting to know more about the circus folk.

Peter and Jack soon managed to get into conversation with the three big men who were so hard at work knocking stakes into the ground.

'Hallo, boys!' the eldest man said kindly. 'You're a bit early, you know – we're not giving a show until tomorrow evening!'

Very soon they found out that this was Mr Kriloff, the circus owner and ringmaster. He was about fifty years old, and he had black hair plastered down over

a bald patch, and a little moustache which he kept on twirling.

The other two, younger men were real giants – but the first thing you noticed about them was how alike they were. They both had clear blue eyes and fair beards.

'Are you brothers?' Peter asked. 'I bet you are!'

'Yes, and not only brothers, we're twins!' said one of the two big men. 'And we do an act as *Siamese* twins in the circus!' said the other, laughing.

'Goodness – however do you do that?' asked Jack, puzzled.

'Ah, that was one of my own bright ideas!' Mr Kriloff told him. 'You see, real Siamese twins would draw a big crowd – so every evening Ivan and Alexander here put on the same huge pair of trousers and clown around in it, back to back. Of course, it's a specially made pair of trousers, with four legs – and everyone can see they're not really Siamese twins, but I can tell you, their comic turn is always a great success!'

Mr Kriloff was twirling his moustache all the time he spoke.

Some way off, on the steps of the caravan, Janet and Barbara were deep in conversation with the fair-haired girl.

'My name's Alice,' she told them, 'and my father runs this circus! Those two boys you can see over there, unfolding the tent, are my brothers. The big one is called Sergei, and the younger one is Boris.'

'It must be so exciting, living in a circus!' said Janet. She was fascinated!

'Yes, I wouldn't change with anyone!' said the little girl proudly.

'And you can watch every performance free – aren't you lucky?' said Barbara.

'Oh, do you think so?' said Alice, laughing. Then she became more serious, and added. 'Actually, I do my *own* turn every evening! It's the number directly after the interval.'

'*You* do a turn,' cried the two girls in chorus.

'Yes – an exhibition of acrobatics on the flying trapeze. You'll see me if you come to one of our performances.'

The two girls immediately promised that they certainly *would* be coming to one of the circus shows.

Out in the middle of the field, Sergei, Boris and Colin were getting on quite well with unfolding the Big Top. They had a nice, smooth expanse of canvas laid out on the ground, and by now the three boys were firm friends. Sergei and Boris were telling Colin about life in the circus.

'We live in that big caravan, with Ivan and Alexander, the twins. My father and mother and Alice live in the white one – over there, where you can see the girls talking.

'What about all the circus equipment?' asked Colin.

'That goes in the big van with the costumes,' replied Sergei.

Colin looked at the van. It had a red loudspeaker shaped like a petunia flower on top. That must be the van Jack had seen going past his house two days before!

As for Pam, she was still watching the fat woman – with so much interest that the woman noticed her, and offered her a plate of delicious hot chips.

'Oh – thank you!' said Pam, feeling rather awkward. But then she plucked up her courage, and asked straight out, 'Do you cook the meals for *all* the circus people?'

The fat woman laughed in a jolly way, and the little bun of hair she wore on top of her head shook as if it might fall off.

'I'm the circus owner's wife, dearie – we all share in the work here. I do the cooking and sell the tickets – *and* I do a clairvoyant act too!'

Pam didn't quite dare to ask what a clairvoyant act was. Anyway, she knew she'd find out if she went to see one of the shows. Meanwhile she was really enjoying Mrs Kriloff's chips.

George was standing by a big trailer labelled MENAGERIE, smiling. A marmoset, behind the bars of its cage, seemed to be bent on doing all it could to attract the boy's attention. It was bouncing about like a rubber ball, hanging by its tail, and then it did acrobatics on its swing and came back to stare at George with big black eyes, baring its teeth as if trying to imitate the boy's laughter. But suddenly there was a great roar from the next cage! The

monkey stopped fooling about. George jumped in alarm – and was astonished to see a savage-looking lion. The lion's vast head with its great yellow mane was a most impressive sight, though George noticed that there was a very sweet, gentle expression in his little black eyes. Fascinated, the boy went closer – and immediately a roar even fiercer than the first one made him retreat in a hurry.

Pam was just finishing her second plate of chips when a little clock in one corner of the caravan began to strike.

'Good gracious – can it be eleven o'clock already?' cried Pam, jumping up.

'Ah, you just don't notice how time passes in a circus!' said Mrs Kriloff, setting to work to beat a dozen egg whites to a stiff frothy meringue.

'I must go! Goodbye, Mrs Kriloff – and thank you very much for the scrumptious chips!'

And Pam ran off.

'Goodbye, dearie!' the jolly, fat woman called after her.

Pam would never win any prizes for punctuality. She had such bad luck! She was always losing her watch, and putting her diary down somewhere and then forgetting where it was! It wasn't *her* fault if she kept on meeting nice people, stopping to talk to them and forgetting all about the time, was it?

'No,' said Pam to herself, 'I can't help it if Mrs Kriloff fries such super chips!'

Then she had to burst into laughter, because she'd spoken out loud, and an old gentleman walking down the road had turned to look at her in great surprise!

Chapter Two

A MEETING OF THE SECRET SEVEN

Pam was still laughing when she reached Peter and Janet's garden, quite breathless. But when she found herself standing outside the door of the shed the smile was soon wiped off her face. Suddenly, she was very worried.

'Oh dear!' she thought. 'I've gone and forgotten the password! What *is* it?'

She searched her pockets frantically, thinking she might have written today's password down, and hoping to find it on a scrap of paper there. No luck! Then she did remember the password – or half-remembered it, because before she could say the word it had partly escaped her again. She knew it was a word beginning with 'water'. Was it 'waterfall?' Or 'waterweed?'

'Waterfall!' she whispered through the keyhole.

No reply.

'Waterweed!' she tried again, not very sure of herself now.

Still the door didn't open.

Poor Pam! If only she didn't have such a sieve-like

memory! Taking a deep breath, she tried all the words beginning with 'water' she could think of.

'Water-lily! Water-rat! Water-boatman! Water polo! Waterloo!'

At last, when she said 'Waterloo!', the door opened. Peter looked sternly at her as she came in, and when he had closed the door after her again he said crossly, 'Next time, Pam, you'll have to copy the password out a hundred times before you leave!'

Pam hung her head, feeling ashamed of herself. George came over to her.

'I know what – next time *Pam* had better choose the password!' he said. 'Then she won't forget it so easily!'

Pam raised her head and smiled at her ally! Scamper, who looked as if he had been following everything, got his own word in by barking loudly.

'Jolly good, Scamper!' said George. 'You agree with me, don't you?'

And that was that. Janet and Barbara came and sat on a bench beside Pam, while the four boys seated themselves on old orange boxes from the grocer's shop.

Jack was the first to speak. 'Peter called this meeting when he found out there was a circus coming here. He wanted us to find out about the show and the circus folk. Well – are you all ready to make your reports?'

'Oh yes!' cried Pam, beaming happily again. 'Listen, I've got a programme for the show! I'll read

20

it out. Then everyone can say what else they know.'

'That's a good idea,' Peter agreed. He was rather sorry he'd been so cross with Pam, and he wanted to make it up to her by being nice.

Pam searched her pockets frantically once more . . . the other six looked at her with foreboding. They were almost sure she'd lost the programme too!

'Don't bother to go on searching!' said Peter, handing her a piece of paper. 'Would *this* by any chance be it?'

'Oh, my programme!' she explained.

'I saw you drop a folded piece of paper outside the door, and when I was letting you in I picked it up.'

'Oh, thank you, Peter!' said Pam, relieved. Then she began reading out what the programme said.

'Number one: Madame Clare the Famous Clair-voyant.'

'Gosh, that sounds like a good start,' said Colin – and he closed his eyes and looked very wise, pretending to be a clairvoyant too.

'What's a clairvoyant?' Janet asked.

'Yes, what *is* a clairvoyant?' Pam wanted to know too.

'It's someone who can tell you things about yourself even if you never met before – in fact someone who can tell you anything you want to know!' explained George.

'Even with her eyes closed!' added Colin, smiling.

'You mean she could tell me the answer to my arithmetic homework?' said Barbara.

'Of course!' replied Peter. 'She could tell you much harder things than that!'

'Well, anyway, it sounds as if we don't want to miss the start,' said Colin, smiling as he looked at Pam.

'I'll make sure I'm there half an hour early!' Pam promised. Then she told them she had actually met Madame Clare. 'She's really Mrs Kriloff the ring-master's wife.'

'And Peter and I have been talking to Mr Kriloff himself,' said Jack. 'He does a horse-riding turn.'

'That must be the second number on the pro-gramme: Viennese Waltz on Horseback,' Pam read out. She went on reading. 'Number three: Miss Daisy the kangaroo shows you what an elegant lady carries in her pouch.'

'Oh, I've seen Miss Daisy the kangaroo,' George told the others. 'She looked rather sweet. There was a monkey in a cage not far from hers, too. He was a real scream – you ought to have seen him!'

George began gesticulating in imitation of the monkey. He jumped up on his orange box, and very nearly tumbled straight off again. Everyone roared with laughter.

'Go on, Pam,' said Peter.

'Number four: Mr Constrictor the Python Man.'

'Oh, that's Sergei' said Colin. 'He's the elder of the two Kriloff brothers. He does an act as a clown too, along with his younger brother Boris.'

'The interval comes next,' said Pam. 'And after that –'

'After that it's Alice!' cried Barbara and Janet in chorus.

'Princess Honey-Bee on her Flying Trapeze!' read Pam.

So then Janet and Barbara told the others about their conversation with Alice, and how 'Princess Honey-Bee' was really Mr and Mrs Kriloff's daughter.

Then Pam read out the title of the sixth number. 'Rico the talking parrot and his silent friend, Tutti-Frutti the marmoset!'

'Oh, that's the monkey I was trying to describe to you just now,' said George – but this time he had the sense to stay put on his orange box!

'Seven: The Musical Clowns.'

'Boris and Sergei,' Colin explained.

'Eight: The Amazing Siamese Twins.'

'We know who *they* are!' said Jack.

'Yes, they're twins all right, but not Siamese ones!' added Peter, smiling. 'We've seen them well and truly separated.'

'And the ninth and last turn,' announced Pam, 'is Brutus the Lion.'

'He looks a really fierce lion, too!' added George, remembering the savage roar that had made him retreat from the animal cages not so long ago.

'I say – it sounds like a super programme,' said Peter, getting up. 'Don't you think so?'

'Yes, it sounds really lovely,' cried the three girls.

'We mustn't miss it!' Jack and Colin agreed.

'When shall we go, then? Thursday or Sunday? Afternoon or evening?' Peter looked round at his friends. They none of them seemed to have any strong feelings.

'Let's vote on it,' suggested Jack.

'All right,' said Janet. 'We girls will get the voting papers ready.'

When everyone had written down the day and time they preferred, and the voting papers had been carefully folded into four, Barbara collected them in an old hat that was lying on a shelf in the shed. Pam counted the votes. There were six votes for Thursday – and one mysterious paper which said, 'Not Thursday, not Sunday, not afternoon, not evening.

'Why not?' asked Pam, rather annoyed.

'Because we haven't got the money for it!' replied the author of this strange paper! It was George, who was the Secret Seven's treasurer and he showed them the little purse he had been clutching.

'Seats cost thirty pence each,' he said, 'and we've only got one pound and twenty pence in the treasury, so there'd only be enough for four of us.'

'We need another ninety pence,' said Pam sadly.

'Oh dear – it doesn't look as if we'll be able to go after all,' said Peter, whistling through his teeth.

'I've got twenty pence – here! I'll do without my comic this week,' said Janet cheerfully.

'And I've got another ten,' said George, taking a shiny coin out of his trouser pocket.

'We still have to find sixty pence,' said Jack.

'No – thirty!' said Colin, smiling. 'Because Boris and Sergei gave me a free ticket for helping them.

Suddenly Scamper the spaniel attracted their attention. 'Woof! Woof!' he barked loudly, waving his plumy tail in the air. 'Woof! Woof!' Then when he was sure they were all taking notice of him, he ran to the end of the shed where his biscuits were kept, and went on barking cheerfully.

'I think he wants us to take the thirty pence out of our funds for his special treats,' said Peter.

'Do you really mean that, Scamper?' asked Janet, patting the dog.

'Woof! Woof!' replied the spaniel, letting his little mistress pet him and licking her hands lovingly.

'Then all we have to do now is get our parents'

permission to go,' said Peter. 'Anyone expect any trouble there?'

Pam put her hand up. 'But if your father could ring up *my* father to persuade him it's all right, and tell him you'd . . . well . . . do you see?'

'We see!' said Colin, smiling. 'Some gallant gentleman, will have to escort you home after the show, right?'

'I don't think *you'll* ever be a very gallant gentleman, Colin!' said Pam offended.

'That'll do!' interrupted Peter. 'We'll *all* escort Pam home, and that's that!'

'Aye, aye, cap'n! Anything you say!' said Jack, standing to attention.

Chapter Three

THE PERFORMANCE

It was pitch dark next evening when the Seven, followed by Scamper, arrived in the field where the circus was being held. The huge Big Top stood out against the sky, looking rather like an enormous bat.

Mrs Kriloff, who was in the ticket office, recognized Pam and gave her very good seats, right in the front row and facing the spot where the performers would come into the ring.

The friends made their way through the crowd of people who had come to watch the performance and took their seats. Only five minutes after they sat down, Jack's sister Susie and her friend Binkie came and sat behind them! The Seven were always trying to keep out of the way of those two little pests – they really did choose the worst possible moments to turn up!

Susie and Binkie pretended not to recognize the Seven, but of course they were watching and listening to everything they said and did. Peter gave Jack a reproachful glance, and Jack replied with a helpless gesture. He leaned over to his friend.

'She must have heard me asking my father for permission to come to the circus this evening,' he whispered.

'Whispering's rude, isn't it, Binkie?' said Susie behind them, and both little girls split their sides laughing.

Janet turned round and asked them quite sharply to be quiet. They laughed louder than ever! The Seven were very relieved when the lights dimmed and the band, positioned up above the performers' entrance, started to play a lively tune.

It was quite dark in the Big Top now. The music was still playing when a little point of light appeared on the velvet curtain. The red velvet moved slightly, the music swelled louder, and the light drew until it was a big, round spotlight. Mr Kriloff stepped into the spotlight, wearing a suit all covered with sparkling sequins. Microphone in hand, he welcomed the audience, and uttered the magic words, 'And now, up with the curtain!'

He went to pull back the red curtains himself, and Mrs Kriloff came out into the ring to do her clairvoyant's act.

Her eyes were blindfolded with a black scarf. It turned out that she could guess all sorts of things right, without ever making a mistake. She told one man in the audience all the numbers and letters on his driving licence, and gave them in the right order too. And she told a lady sitting in the third row back exactly what was in a letter folded up inside her handbag. The Seven were astonished!

Barbara had an idea.

'Why don't we ask her what our last password was?' she suggested in a whisper.

'Let's try!' said Peter, his eyes bright with excitement.

He stood up. Mr Kriloff saw him, and asked him to put his question loud enough for Madame Clare and the whole audience to hear him.

'Right – what was the last password used by the Secret Seven?' he asked in a loud, clear voice.

Mrs Kriloff put her hands to her forehead, as if that would help her to concentrate better.

'I see a name . . . the name of a place,' she said after a few seconds. 'The word has eight letters – am I right?'

'Yes,' said Peter.

'It is something to do with water . . . water . . .'

'Gosh – that's amazing!' cried Peter.

'Wait . . . ah, now I see it! The name is the name of a battlefield . . .' Mrs Kriloff went on. 'It is . . . it is WATERLOO!'

'Quite right!' said Peter. 'Oh, well done!'

All the Seven stood up to applaud – and Scamper joined in too, barking.

Soon afterwards Mrs Kriloff went off again, to the sound of clapping. Then her husband came into the ring and gave a dazzling display of *haute école* on a grey mare with pink feathers on her head. After that, he introduced Miss Daisy the kangaroo, who brought all sorts of things out of her pouch, from a lipstick to a telephone! The small children in the audience loved her act! Then came Sergei Kriloff – or Mr Constrictor the Python Man! Sergei was extremely thin and could coil himself up like a rope or a snake. The climax of his performance was when he squeezed himself into a transparent plastic box no bigger than a suitcase!

Next it was the interval. The lights went on again – and those two pests Susie and Binkie kept on chanting, 'Waterloo, Waterloo, Waterloo!' Jack, very irritated, turned to his sister and told her, 'You needn't think we're going to keep *that* password now everybody knows it!'

'Never mind, I'll find out the next one!' said cheeky Susie. 'I have my methods!' And she cupped her hands above her head and swivelled them round like a radar receiver.

'You think you're as clever as Mrs Kriloff, do you?' said her brother.

'That'll do!' said Peter. 'The show's supposed to be down there in the ring, not a fight up here in the audience!'

Susie shut up at once, and Binkie kept quiet too.

Many of the audience had got up to stretch their legs, but they were already coming back to their seats now. Soon the band struck up a rhythmical march, and in a moment or so the lights went out again. The spectators were murmuring happily, wondering what marvel would come out into the ring next. Suddenly a blinding spotlight shone out in the dark, showing them a slim little girl up at the very top of the tent, poised on a trapeze as if about to take flight! It was Alice, the Kriloffs' daughter. She was a glittering sight in her golden costume, with a circlet round her forehead and two antennae made of fake diamonds on it. She had two little wings of tulle embroidered with gold and silver on her back. Alice really did look like a honey-bee hanging from the trapeze by her hands and feet and swinging across the tent, going farther and faster each time, and brushing past a huge artificial rose about thirty feet above the ground every time she flew one side of the tent to the other.

Suddenly all the music stopped except for a dramatic drum-roll. That was the only accompaniment of Alice's breathtaking and dangerous display.

At the microphone, Mr Kriloff asked the audience for complete silence. All eyes were riveted to the young artiste. Barbara and Janet were more excited than anyone! Barbara was nervously twisting her hands, and Janet had to bite her lips hard. Suddenly, cries of amazement rang through the tent. At the very highest point of her flight, Alice had simply let go of her trapeze – and she landed lightly and gracefully in the very heart of the rose! Then all the spotlights were turned on the middle of the ring. The audience clapped and clapped. The rose sank down to floor level, and Alice stepped out of its petals. She took a bow – and had to come back several times to acknowledge the cheers for her performance.

The next number was the act performed by Rico the parrot and Tutti-Frutti the marmoset. The two of them were so funny when they got covered with shaving cream! After that Sergei Kriloff and his brother Boris gave the younger members of the audience a real treat. Dressed as clowns, they chased

each other in turn, brandishing an outsize violin! Then the audience had the fun of seeing Ivan and Alexander, the amazing Siamese twins, getting out of a big velvet-lined trunk! Of course it was obvious that they were not real Siamese twins, and everyone laughed as Mr Kriloff told the dramatic tale of their travels – but they were so clever at moving about in time with each other, just as if they really *were* joined together! When one of them moved forwards, the other followed him at precisely the right moment, but moving backwards – and the other way around!

The Seven smiled and laughed as they watched their new friends perform.

Then it was to be the grand finale. Some men came in and set up the lion's cage. Its bars were all in place in less that five minutes.

Boris, the young lion-tamer, got a round of applause when he walked into the cage. He was wearing a red coat with gold braid on it, white breeches, and black leather boots. He stood there alone, a whip in his hand, waiting for Brutus the lion.

But the minutes passed by, and no lion appeared in the mouth of the narrow tunnel leading straight into the cage. Boris filled in time by making sure the stools on which the lion would soon be jumping were nice and steady.

By now the spectators were beginning to get impatient. Suddenly, someone yelled Brutus's name, and soon they were all chanting, 'Brutus, Brutus! We want Brutus!'

The Seven, sitting in the front row, were wondering what had happened. They suspected something was badly wrong.

'This is really odd, you know!' shouted Colin, making his cupped hands into a loudspeaker so that the others could hear him through all the din the audience was making.

'Perhaps Brutus has escaped!' said Jack.

'Oh no – don't even *say* such an awful thing!' said Janet. She was already terrified!

'Good, here comes Mr Kriloff!' said Peter. 'Now the show will go on.'

But the ringmaster was looking very worried as he came out into the ring. 'Unfortunately,' he announced gloomily, 'Brutus, the famous King of the Jungle Circus, will not be able to appear this evening.'

A murmur of disappointment ran through the audience. Mr Kriloff raised his right hand for silence, and went on, 'Brutus the lion is suffering from bronchitis and has a high temperature. Those who want may have their money back – and anyone else can come to see the show again, free, on Sunday, at either the afternoon or the evening performance. Ask for tickets or your money back as you go out – and I can promise you,' he added, forcing himself to smile, 'that in three days' time, when Brutus is better, he will scare the living daylights out of you!'

Chapter Four

A LION AT LARGE

The disappointed spectators got up and went to the exit. What an anti-climax! However, most of them were going to get their free tickets for one of the Sunday performances. But back in the fourth row on the left, one voice shouted out angrily, 'Scandalous! I call it a shame – a crying shame! Really, I've never known anything like it! Barefaced robbery, that's what it is!'

It was Mr Chapman, who owned a big chemist's shop not far away. He sounded very cross indeed, but nobody was surprised. He was well known locally for his bad temper! As it turned out, he was the only member of the audience who insisted on having his money back!

As soon as Mr Kriloff had made his announcement, Peter had sent George off to find out more, if he could. Now the six others were waiting for George near the entrance. George had some difficulty getting back to them, because he had to make his way through a crowd of people waiting at the ticket office.

But he waved to them from the other side of the queue.

'I wonder what he's trying to tell us?' said Barbara. Suddenly she felt very worried.

'Nothing too good, by the look of him!' said Jack.

At last George rejoined them. 'It's dreadful!' he began. He was panting for breath, because he had been running.

Jack couldn't wait to know what had really happened. 'Has Brutus escaped?' he asked.

'Yes, he *has*!' gasped George, still quite over-whelmed by the news he had heard. 'Apparently Tutti-Fruttie, the little monkey, somehow unbolted the door of his cage during Ivan and Alexander's act!'

'That's incredible!' said Peter, whistling through his teeth.

'But it happened! Mr Kriloff told me it was something nobody could have foreseen,' George went on. 'The bolt was a very, very heavy one – he didn't think the marmoset *could* push it back!'

'I read somewhere that monkeys have tremen-dously strong muscles,' said Jack.

'Oh, but this is awful!' cried Pam, suddenly realizing the danger. 'Just think – we could all be eaten alive!'

'Calm down and don't panic,' Peter told her reassuringly.

'Still, the public will have to be warned,' said Colin firmly.

'Yes – people must barricade themselves inside

their houses,' Janet agreed. She was already on the verge of panic herself.

'We'd better warn the audience at once, while there's still time,' suggested Barbara.

'Oh no – please don't,' said a little voice behind them.

The Seven turned round and saw Alice, the clever young trapeze artiste. She was still wearing her acrobat's costume, though she had put a black wool shawl round her shoulders.

'If you tell everyone there really *will* be panic!' she said, coming over to the children.

'But a lion on the loose *is* dangerous!' said Peter firmly.

'No, honestly, Brutus is as gentle as a lamb – even

gentler!' Alice explained, tears in her eyes. 'He's a most unusual lion! He hates meat – in fact, his favourite food is sweetcorn! If the people here know he's run away, they're sure to organize a lion hunt to track him down, and some of them will have guns – and since Brutus is so friendly and hasn't an ounce of vice in him, he'll just walk up to someone and get himself killed!'

Alice was sobbing so hard that she couldn't say any more. Janet and Barbara hugged her and promised they would help.

'Listen, Alice – all the Secret Seven are here!' said Barbara. 'You remember how we were telling you about our secret society the other day?'

One by one the members of the Secret Seven introduced themselves.

'And this is Scamper, the best dog in the world,' said Peter, taking the dog in his arms.

The spaniel licked Alice's hands comfortingly, just as if he knew she was upset.

'Now – how can we help you and your family?' asked Jack.

'Let's go over to the animals' cages,' said Alice.

A great many of the spectators were still surrounding the menagerie trailer. They all wanted a glimpse of Brutus, the famous lion, who had not been able to appear that evening. But they were doomed to disappointment: the lion's cage was covered by a big tarpaulin.

Mr Kriloff and his sons were trying to get the

crowd to go away, telling them Brutus needed peace
and quiet if he was to get better. The Seven stationed
themselves at several strategic points around the
trailer, to stop the naughty little boys who kept trying
to lift the tarpaulin and steal a look at the sick lion.

At last, after about an hour, the inquisitive
onlookers lost interest and went home. Mr Kriloff
thanked the Seven for being so helpful – and then he
got ready to set off in search of the missing lion.

'I'm sure everything will be all right again in a
couple of hours' time,' he said, smiling.

'Yes, I bet Brutus is just having a quiet nap in
somebody's garden!' Boris agreed.

Sergei joined them, bringing several big electric
torches. Alice hugged the girls goodnight and went
into her caravan. Then the Seven said goodnight to
all the other circus folk.

On their way home, the children turned round
after they had gone a little way, and saw the beams of
three powerful torches being shone into one dark
garden after another.

One by one the party of children dispersed.
Barbara and George were the first to get home, then
Jack and Colin. Finally, after seeing Pam right to her
own doorstep, Peter and Janet set off for the
farmhouse.

Suddenly they heard a fire engine's bell clanging
through the night! The two children saw the
reflection of its flashing light on the houses – and then
not one but *three* red fire engines came dashing round

the corner of the road! Peter and Janet started running to see where the fire was. When they reached the crossroads, Peter cried, 'Look – it's over there! See all that smoke behind the clock tower?'

They soon reached the church. The village garage stood nearby – and it had gone up in flames. But the firemen were already directing their hoses on the blaze, and soon the whole place was running with water. Dozens of firemen's hoses, all tangled up together, were playing on the fire, and in half an hour's time it was out.

It turned out that there was not too much harm done after all, though it had been a frightening incident. Peter and Janet could see people standing at windows in their nightclothes, talking about what had happened. It was late by now, and the two children went away.

'All that noise and commotion won't have made things any easier for the Kriloffs!' said Peter thoughtfully.

Janet only yawned. Poor girl – she *was* so tired!

When they got home they were surprised to see lights on all over the house. Mother was waiting up for them, and she looked very worried, because she had expected them much earlier. Peter explained about Brutus, and the fire at the garage, and then he went up to his bedroom. As for Janet, she was already fast asleep in hers!

Chapter Five

THE LION HUNT BEGINS

The Seven got up rather earlier than usual next morning. They wanted to go to the circus field before school, and find out if there was any news.

Mr Kriloff was looking very downcast. 'I'm sorry to say we haven't found Brutus yet,' he told them. 'When those fire engines went past last night with their bells clanging they must have scared him away. We searched all night – no luck!'

During the school dinner hour, Peter and Jack went back to the circus field again, but there was still no news – and no trace of Brutus!

As they walked back to school, Peter suggested calling a special meeting of the Seven when lessons were over.

'We simply must help the Kriloffs,' he said. 'After all, what *will* they do if Brutus hasn't been found by Sunday?'

So at five o'clock, after a very hasty tea, the Seven all met, and Peter led them straight off to the Jungle Circus, where they found the Kriloff family all

together in one of the two caravans. They were
discussing the situation. The children's arrival
lightened the atmosphere a bit – the circus folk had
been feeling very dismal all day long.

'Mr Kriloff,' said Peter directly, 'we've come to
offer you our help. We're a pretty good team, you
know – we've formed ourselves into a society called
the Secret Seven, and we've solved all sorts of
mysterious problems already!'

'Come along in, children!' said Mr Kriloff,
smiling. 'It may be a bit crowded round this little
table, but we're all friends here, and glad to see you!'

Mrs Kriloff poured them out some orange juice, and Alice put a tin of biscuits on the table. Boris, the young lion-tamer, turned to the children.

'You see, I know old Brutus,' he told them, 'and he really wouldn't hurt a fly! He must have been frightened by all the noise yesterday evening, and he'll have run away into the nearby countryside.'

'Well – we know these parts pretty well,' said Jack. 'We could guide you round.'

'Would it be all right to take Scamper?' asked Peter. 'Or would that scare Brutus?'

'Oh no!' replied Boris. 'Brutus likes dogs – he was reared with a litter of puppies.'

Offering her friends more biscuits, Alice told them how Rico the parrot was great friends with the lion too. 'He spends whole days perched on Brutus's back, catching his fleas for him!' she said. Then she turned to her father, and added, 'Dad – suppose we took Rico with us, *he* might be able to help!'

'That's not a bad idea, Alice!' said Mr Kriloff.

At last Peter got to his feet, and the others followed suit.

'Well then, that's settled, Mr Kriloff. We're not free tomorrow morning, because we're all taking part in a school concert, but if you still haven't got Brutus back we'll come round in the afternoon and help you to search.'

'Thanks, lad – thanks a lot, all of you! But I hope we shan't need your help! I'm hoping and praying it will all be over by tomorrow morning, because we really can't conceal Brutus's disappearance much longer. He'll draw attention to himself before long – and then he'll have the police after him . . .'

Poor Mr Kriloff's voice trailed miserably away, but he forced himself to smile at the children.

The Seven said goodbye to the circus folk, and Alice hugged the three girls as if they were sisters. Then the children went home, but before they said goodbye to each other, Peter called a meeting for one-thirty next day.

So at one-thirty on Saturday afternoon, the Seven met near the circus field. Peter was having some difficulty keeping Scamper in order – the golden spaniel was bounding around everywhere.

'He can smell adventure in the air!' Peter told the others.

Mr Kriloff and Alice soon joined them outside the entrance of the Big Top. As soon as the Seven saw their faces, they felt sure the news was still bad.

'No sign of him yet,' said Mr Kriloff, shaking hands with them. 'We haven't had a wink of sleep all night. Sergei and Boris and I combed three miles of woodland to the north and east of this village – but there wasn't the slightest trace of Brutus!'

'Then it's up to us!' said Peter cheerfully. 'We plan to separate into two groups, Mr Kriloff, to save time. Jack will lead the first group, and take the three girls, while Colin and I have Alice, Scamper and Rico the parrot with us.'

'Hey, how about me?' asked George. 'You've left me out!'

'You must stay here to keep us all in touch. We'll be using those walkie-talkie radio sets my father gave us last Christmas. Jack and I will have one each, and you hang on to the third, George. Then you can let us know about anything that happens here while we're gone. And if we do need any help, you'll have to tell Mr Kriloff and his sons – they'll be getting some rest after their tiring night! Well – got it?'

'Got it!' said Jack and George in chorus.

They decided that Jack's team would search the meadows to the south of the circus field, because Barbara and Pam knew them very well – they'd often been to pick mushrooms there! Peter and Alice and Colin would explore the wooded country over to the west.

When everything was ready and everyone knew what to do, the Seven set off, taking Alice and Rico with them. First they went to Peter and Janet's house to pick up the walkie-talkies, and then, after wishing each other good luck, they separated as they had agreed.

As soon as they were away from the houses, Jack and the three girls hurried as fast as they could, and soon they reached a little hill. From the top they could get a fine view of the country round about.

'I don't see Brutus anywhere!' said Pam. She was already tired of walking.

'Oh – looked right behind all those hedges, have

you!' Jack asked her, pointing at them.

'Come on, Pam!' said Barbara. 'It's downhill all the way now – let's go!'

And she ran down the slope, full tilt. The other three followed, and caught up with her by the first hedge. They pushed aside the branches of the hedgerow and made their way through it. They found themselves in a little meadow, with a large black and white cow grazing peacefully in it.

'Well, no lions here – unless that's Brutus under a magic spell!' said Janet, laughing.

Then they went on to the next meadow. Since they found nothing there either, they tried the next one – and so it went on for a least half an hour.

Jack looked at his watch and then switched on the walkie-talkie.

'George and Peter must be wondering what we're up to,' he said, pulling out the aerial.

The three girls came close to him, so that they could hear the conversation too.

'Hallo – Jack speaking! Jack speaking! Over!'

'Receiving you loud and clear, Jack,' George answered. 'What news?'

'No news at all. This area seems to be clear. How are you doing?'

'Oh, all's quiet here at the circus field.'

'Hallo, Jack! Peter speaking! Are you there, Jack?' Peter was joining in the conversation over his own walkie-talkie.

'Hallo, Peter,' said Jack. 'Have *you* discovered anything?'

'No, not a thing. We're going very slowly because . . .' But here he was interrupted by a crackling sound over the radio sets, which went on for several minutes.

'Hallo?' said Peter, when it stopped. 'As I was saying, we're making very slow progress because the wood is so thick.'

'Message received,' said Jack. 'We'll call you again in . . .' But once more the conversation was interrupted by interference noises, and at the same moment a flash of lightning streaked across the sky.

'Lightning!' cried Pam. 'That noise on our radio set means there's a storm coming!'

'Then we won't be able to use them any more!' said Barbara, rather worried. However, a few moments later they were back in touch again.

'It looks as if we're in for quite a storm,' Jack told Peter and George. 'So I'm signing off for the time being!' And he broke contact.

It certainly *was* quite a storm that suddenly broke over the countryside – more of a deluge, in fact. Jack and the three girls ran as fast as they could to shelter under a hedge. Unfortunately the bushes had few leaves left on them at this time of year, so they didn't give much protection. The rain lasted only a few minutes, but that was quite long enough for the four friends to get soaked to the skin!

When the sky was clear again Jack got back in touch with George.

'Hallo, George!' he said. He was shivering with cold. 'Listen, I'm afraid we've got to give up – we're knee-deep in water! We're coming back – anyone who wants to search around here any more will have to do it by boat!'

Just then Peter joined the radio conversation too.

'That's all right, Jack,' he said. 'You come back. We were luckier than you were – we found a forester's hut where we could keep dry! Oh, here's Alice, and she wants a word with you.'

'Please don't worry,' said Alice. 'If Brutus ever *was* in those meadows I'm sure he isn't there any longer – the rain will have made him run for it!'

'Well, see you this evening!' said Peter, before signing off.

Jack and the girls went home to get dry, wading through meadows which were more like marshes now. Meanwhile the others were still searching the woods. Gloomily, Peter looked at the undergrowth, dripping with water after the rain.

'We're out of luck,' he said. 'Scamper will never be able to pick up a scent on ground that's so soaked with water!'

'Let's try him once again,' Colin suggested.

So Alice bent down to put Brutus's muzzle and chain under the spaniel's nose – the idea was to get the dog used to the lion's scent.

'Go on, sniff it – good dog!' said Peter, patting him.

50

Scamper spent quite a long time nosing around the muzzle, as if he hoped to find something interesting inside it. Then his master gave the word to start out, and the little party set off again. Alice walked behind the two boys with the green parrot perched on one shoulder.

The paths they took became quite swampy in places, and it was difficult to make much progress. 'Ah, well, there's always a bright side!' said Jack suddenly. 'The rain certainly made things harder for Scamper, but just look at the fine tracks we're leaving!' And he pointed to their footprints in the mud behind them.

'You're right', said Peter, cheering up. 'Wherever Brutus goes, *he'll* leave the tracks behind him too!'

'Then the storm was a good thing after all!' cried Alice, smiling happily.

This discovery of theirs made all three of them feel much more cheerful. Suddenly they heard George's voice over the walkie-talkie.

'Hallo, Peter – Peter, can you hear me?'

'Yes, receiving you loud and clear!' said Peter.

'Something's happened – something really important!' shouted George, sounding very excited. 'I've really got some news this time!'

'Well, come on, then, tell us!' said Peter impatiently. He wished George would get to the point.

'OK, here you are – Brutus has actually been sighted, less than twenty minutes ago, in the kitchen of the Blue Boar hotel! He must have been attracted to it by the smell of cooking, because he tried to steal something to eat, and upset a big saucepan that was standing on the stove. He must have burnt himself, poor thing, because apparently he roared very loudly – and then he went into the dining room. The people who'd been eating in there had run away in panic, so he licked all their plates clean! Even the manager of the Blue Boar didn't dare go back inside the hotel to telephone – he jumped into his car and went to raise the alarm. Golly, you should have seen him! He was white as a sheet when he dashed into the police station. It was the police who told me all this!'

'Then is Brutus still at the Blue Boar?' asked Peter excitedly.

'Hang on a minute, I haven't finished yet! No – the police rang up the hotel, and one of the customers there answered the phone and told them Brutus had gone away again.'

'Which way did he go?'

'Towards Deep Dingle.'

'Good! Listen – we'll be at Deep Dingle in five minutes' time, and you must keep your ears pricked for anything you hear people say, George. We're setting off this minute.'

And Peter broke radio contact, folded away the aerial of his set and gave the others the signal to leave. Scamper ran ahead of them as they struck across country and made for the valley known as Deep Dingle as fast as they could go.

Chapter Six

IN DEEP DINGLE

Alice was terribly worried. She had been afraid something like this would happen ever since Brutus disappeared – and now it *had* happened. The lion had been seen, so the police knew that he was on the loose! Now they would mount a big operation, and he would be lucky to escape alive. She was lost in these sad thoughts when Colin called, 'Here we are! This is Deep Dingle!'

Peter and Alice joined him and looked down at the valley opening out below them. A steep path down one side led to the bottom of Deep Dingle. Carefully, Peter began climbing down, giving Alice a hand so that she would not fall. Colin brought up the rear, carrying Scamper.

At last, after fifteen minutes' tricky climb down, the three friends reached the bottom of the valley. It was narrow and full of brushwood. At one end of Deep Dingle was a blank rock wall. A beautiful waterfall cascaded down there in springtime. At the other end, the valley fell away to more level country-side.

'Let's go straight to the steep end of the valley first,'

suggested Peter 'If we find nothing there we'll retrace our steps and go on out into the country.'

Soon they reached the end of the ravine, where the two sides of the valley met in a steep, rocky wall. 'Goodness – it's almost like a cave in among those rocks!' said Alice in surprise.

'You ought to see the lovely waterfall that comes down here in spring,' Peter told her. He pointed to the top of the rocks. A few drops of water from the afternoon's storm were trickling down.

'This is all very well,' grumbled Colin, 'but I don't see any sign of Brutus about.'

So the three of them – and Scamper – set off again, going all the way down Deep Dingle. They kept abreast, moving farther away from each other as the valley grew wider, so that no possible hiding place would escape their sharp eyes!

They had only just passed the end of the steep path down which they had climbed into the valley, when they saw a patch of disturbed earth on the side of the slope.

'Looks as if somebody's been this way quite recently,' said Peter.

'Brutus!' cried Alice, running towards the spot.

She couldn't really have known, and was speaking on impulse – or perhaps out of wishful thinking. But in a moment it turned out she was right.

'Look – it *was* Brutus! He's left his tracks everywhere!' she told the boys excitedly as they came up.

Peter whistled. 'I say! Footprints – or do I mean pawprints? That's wonderful!'

'*He* didn't take the easier long way down into the valley, any more than we did,' Colin agreed, looking at the earth and stones Brutus had churned up as he ran down the steep slope.

'Well, since he isn't down here any more he must have made for open country,' said Peter 'It would have been too difficult for him to climb *up* this steep slope again.'

'And he was here less than an hour ago,' Colin pointed out. 'We can work that out, because he left his prints in the muddy ground *after* the rain!'

'Oh, how wonderful to think that . . . to think that . . .' Alice began, and then couldn't finish her sentence! She was so excited to think her beloved Brutus was not far off.

The two boys couldn't help laughing, and Alice laughed too! All three of them felt very relieved all of a sudden. They had had two days of such anxiety, but now they were really hopeful once more.

'Well, there's no time to be lost,' said Peter, sounding serious again. 'Come on, Scamper, show us what you can do!'

The spaniel sniffed hard at Brutus's prints, and then he went off, nose to the ground, followed by the three children.

Before long they heard a crackling sound from the walkie-talkie which Peter was carrying slung over his shoulder. It was George, wanting to get in touch and deliver a message. Peter listened as he walked on.

'There's just been an announcement about the missing lion over the radio,' said George. 'The newsreader said the police wanted anyone who had seen Brutus to report the sighting to the nearest police station at once.'

'Message received and understood – thanks,' replied Peter. 'And listen, we're on the right track!' he told George. 'We've found fresh prints, made by Brutus not long ago, and Scamper's on his trail at this very moment.'

'Oh, jolly good!' said George, over the walkie-talkie. 'Well, good luck, Peter, and see you soon!'

Peter signed off again. By now Scamper had led the three friends back to the little path which wound its way along the bottom of the valley, and they found more prints in the muddy ground. Then the spaniel shot off into the brushwood again. The children could not follow Brutus's trail themselves any more, as no prints showed on the thick carpet of dead leaves, but the dog, with his keen sense of smell, could still pick up the lion's scent.

Suddenly Colin uttered an exclamation of surprise.

'Look – there he is!' he cried.

'Where?' asked Peter and Alice at the same moment, in great excitement.

'Over there – behind that thorn bush!' And Colin pointed the spot out to his friends. Sure enough, they too saw a light-coloured patch, the colour of a lion, behind the branches and the brambles in their way.

Alice ran towards the bushes, but the sound of her footsteps must have frightened the lion, because the yellow shape melted into the undergrowth and disappeared.

'Oh, Brutus – poor, dear old Brutus!' she called,

very disappointed.

'You went too fast,' Peter told her.

'Let's climb part of the way up the slope,' suggested Colin. 'We ought to be able to see him then.'

No sooner said than done! Cautiously, the three friends scrambled a little way back up the steep slope again, far enough to get a good view of the whole of Deep Dingle below them. And sure enough . . . .

'There he is again!' cried Alice, delighted. 'Rico – off you go, and tell him we've come to take him home to the circus!'

With a practised gesture, she threw the green parrot up into the air. Like an arrow, Rico made straight for the lion, who was bounding away towards the wide end of the valley now. A moment later some thick bushes hid both the lion and the parrot from the children's sight.

'Well, let's climb back down,' said Peter. 'Now he has his friend the parrot with him, I'm sure Brutus will feel less nervous.'

Alice was smiling broadly as she thought of her father and brothers, and how pleased they would be when she brought the lion back.

As they were starting off to follow Brutus and Rico, Colin said in surprise, 'Hallo, where's old Scamper? I can't see him!'

'He went after Brutus just now, when I ran towards him,' said Alice.

Peter suddenly turned very pale. 'Gosh . . . do you suppose . . . ?' he began.

Alice guessed what he was thinking, and burst out

laughing. 'Peter you don't think for a moment that Brutus has *eaten* him, do you? Why, if they're together, I bet they're having a fine game, rolling about on the ground or chasing each other in a friendly way. Brutus wouldn't hurt your dog, honestly he wouldn't so don't worry!'

They went on searching, but they found nothing. It was getting quite dark by the time they left the valley, and still they had not seen the lion, the dog or the parrot again. Peter decided they would have to stop hunting now, but since Rico and Scamper were probably with the lion, there was a very good chance of finding him quickly in the morning.

On their way back, George made radio contact with them again as they were approaching the village. 'Listen – here's the latest urgent piece of news!' he said. 'Four coach-loads of policemen will arrive in the village before dawn tomorrow, and the police are going to search the whole countryside, using dogs. Some of them will be armed with guns to shoot anaesthetic darts!'

'Shoot?' cried Alice, looking very upset. She didn't know just what George meant, but the idea was alarming.

'Only the kind of dart that sends animals to sleep,' Peter explained. 'Vets use them out in the bush, so that they can give medical help to the big game there.'

Alice was reassured – for a moment she had feared the police were planning to kill Brutus.

Once again Peter heard George's voice, though very faintly, as if something was muffling it. Peter had to put the walkie-talkie right against his ear.

'Listen, Peter, can you get farther away from Alice, so she doesn't catch any of what I say?' George asked.

Peter slowed down, and let the other two pass him. 'OK, George,' he said. 'You can speak freely!'

'All right,' said George, still in a low voice. 'Listen – our dear friend Mr Chapman the chemist has been telling anyone who'll listen to him that *he* intends to go lion-hunting tomorrow too. And he said he'd know what to do if he met "that maneater" – he'd pepper him with buckshot and have his skin for a bedside rug!'

'Right – the Secret Seven meet in half an hour's time!' said Peter. 'Pass it on to the others.'

'They're here with me – where shall we meet?'

'In the shed.'

'How about "Chapman" for a password? That was Pam's idea!'

'A jolly good idea, too,' said Peter. 'See you soon, then!'

And a little later the three children arrived in the village. The two boys said goodbye to Alice and promised to meet her at six next morning.

'I'm sure Brutus will be back roaring happily in his cage tomorrow afternoon!' said Peter, as they parted.

'How wonderful that would be!' sighed Alice. She didn't sound really convinced.

Chapter Seven

A SERIOUS SITUATION

At seven o'clock that evening the Secret Seven met in the shed at the bottom of Peter and Janet's garden. No sooner had they sat down on the upturned orange boxes than there was a knock at the door. Although they had all arrived already, Peter automatically asked, 'Password?'

'Chapman,' said a little voice on the other side of the door.

The head of the Secret Seven suddenly turned to look at his friends in dismay – he realized what this meant! There were six of them there, so it wasn't one of *them* asking to come in! Who could it be? And how did someone else come to know the right password?

Feeling very angry, Peter flung open the door – and saw Alice there!

'Who told you our password?' he shouted.

The poor girl was trembling all over and couldn't say a word.

'I did!' said Pam, getting to her feet. 'Alice saw me running down the road, and called out to me. I pretended not to hear – but she's a jolly good, fast runner, and she soon caught up with me.'

'You see, I guessed something was going on,' said Alice, calming down a bit. 'And Pam told me you were holding a special, important meeting, and you wouldn't let me in unless I knew the password.'

'So you told her, did you?' interrupted Peter, turning to Pam.

Pam looked defiant, as much as to say, 'What would *you* have done in my place?'

'Traitor!' said Colin angrily.

Alice, who was still standing in the doorway, couldn't bear to hear this. 'Oh, please don't be horrid to Pam!' she said. 'It was all my fault – and I can see you think of me as an enemy.'

'No, we don't,' said Peter. 'But you must try to understand – our secret society isn't any good unless we all keep the rules, and it's up to me to make sure we do! Still, just for once I'll let you attend our meeting!'

Alice thanked Peter, and went to sit between Barbara and Janet. Peter carefully closed the door again and told the others what he had decided they ought to do.

'As soon as this meeting's over, Barbara and Pam will go and see Mr Chapman on their way home and try to make him change his mind. And George, Colin and Jack will go to the police station and tell our friend the inspector about Mr Chapman's threat to kill Brutus. As for you, Alice, you must promise here and now not to say a word about any of this to your family – except Boris. Since he's the lion-tamer, we'll let him come with us tomorrow.'

Alice promised to do just as Peter said.

'Well, the sun rises at six tomorrow,' Peter went on. 'I looked in the paper, and it said so there. Now, I want you all to meet here outside the garden gate at five-thirty. Anyone who's late will just be left behind. Let's all set our watches to show the same time – I make it exactly twenty-eight minutes past seven now.'

Peter and Janet didn't need their alarm clock next morning – they were woken up about half past four by Scamper's frantic barking. The poor dog was out in the road, the front door of the house was closed, and he was getting very impatient. Peter went straight down to let him in.

'Ssh! Everyone's asleep,' Peter whispered. 'Where *have* you been, you bad dog?'

Scamper's only reply was to rub against his master's legs. He was wet with the morning dew – and his coat smelled of lion!

'You've been spending the night with Brutus, haven't you?' said Peter. 'In that case you'll be able to lead us to him!'

The spaniel frisked around his young master to show that he understood, and then made for the door, ready to set off at once.

'Wait a minute, old chap! We're not leaving just yet – soon, though!'

The Seven all met outside Peter and Janet's house at the agreed time. Alice and her brother Boris were the first to arrive. They neither of them wanted to miss such an exciting expedition.

However, Jack was very nearly late. He came running up just as the others were about to set of.

'Someone's stolen my walkie-talkie!' he cried breathlessly. 'I turned my whole room upside down before I left – I just can't find it anywhere!'

Peter wasn't going to waste any time over that just now. 'I expect you'll find it this evening,' he said. 'But anyway, we've got the other two, so come on!'

Scamper led the children back towards Deep Dingle in the early morning mists. As they walked along, they made their reports on the missions Peter had sent them to carry out the evening before.

'Mr Chapman was very cross and nasty,' Pam said.

'Yes,' Barbara agreed. 'He simply wouldn't listen to us. The moment we mentioned Brutus he slammed the door in our faces!'

'*We* didn't get much of a hearing at the police station either,' said Jack. Colin nodded.

'No, the inspector didn't seem to be taking Mr Chapman's threat very seriously,' added George.

The nine friends were nearly out of the village when a distant sound made them stop. 'Oh, what is it?' cried Alice, turning to look back at the houses. That was the way the noise was coming from.

'Motor engines!' said Boris. 'Several of them, I think.'

'It must be the coaches full of policemen!' said Peter. 'They've reached the village already! We'd better hurry – we haven't got much of a start!'

And as they set off again, they heard a loudspeaker announcement echoing through the village streets. 'This is a police warning! Everyone in the village must stay indoors. Whatever you do, do not come out. A lion has escaped from the Jungle Circus. When we have caught it, we shall sound sirens to give you the all clear. Attention, please! This is a police warning! Everyone in the village . . .'

The police message was broadcast at least ten times. The children just stood there listening to the disembodied, sinister-sounding voice for several minutes. The village houses looked a bit like a fortress in the mist, and it was a rather frightening sight.

Then the words of the loudspeaker announcement suddenly changed – and they roused the children to action!

'Calling Mr Chapman, we repeat, Mr Chapman! Will Mr Chapman please go to the police station without delay? Calling Mr Chapman!'

'My goodness, you were wrong, George!' cried Peter. 'They *did* take Mr Chapman's threat seriously, all right! Well, come on, or we haven't a chance of being first on the scene!'

They set off at the double to make up for lost time.

George put on a spurt to catch up with Peter, who was in the lead. He wanted to tell Peter about something he'd seen that very morning.

'Listen – before I met you all just now, I thought I saw our friend the big game hunter walking down the road!'

'You mean Mr Chapman?' asked Peter.

'You bet I mean Mr Chapman! He was carrying a gun slung over his shoulder, and he had his dog with him on a leash.'

'Where was he going?'

'The same way as us – and he must be well ahead of us by now!'

'Well, don't worry,' Peter told him. 'After all, *we've* got Scamper! But I think it would be best not to let the others know!'

'What are you two talking about?' asked Alice, catching up with the two boys.

'Oh, I was just telling George not to worry because we've got Scamper with us!' said Peter. And at the sound of his name the spaniel pricked up his ears and began running faster, as if encouraged by all this interest in him!

Chapter Eight

THOSE TWO PESTS!

Once they were off the road and out in open country, Peter let Scamper off his lead and Alice showed him Brutus's muzzle. The spaniel sniffed at it for quite a long time, and then bounded off through the thickets. The children had to go a good deal faster than before to follow him. Peter, George and Boris went straight to the head of the procession, closely followed by Alice and Janet. Behind them, Pam and Barbara were having trouble keeping up, and Jack and Colin kept urging them on.

As they went along, they were all thinking about what they were already calling 'the Brutus affair', and discussing it with the others. Jack was still wondering who could have gone off with his walkie-talkie – that made things even more complicated! But the question that came up most often was whether or not Mr Chapman the chemist had gone to the police station, as he had been asked to do. Only George and Peter knew the truth, and the others, who didn't, were developing all sorts of theories.

'He may have left before that message came over the loudspeaker,' said Colin.

'And even if he *was* still in the village,' said Pam, 'he *may* have gone to the police station – but then again he may have taken no notice, and gone off lion-hunting as he planned!'

'In other words,' said Alice, gloomily, 'the odds are that he's after Brutus at this very moment.'

'However, he doesn't know where to search,' Janet pointed out. 'He's in the dark, and we aren't!'

'You've forgotten his dog,' said Jack. 'He has a very good tracker dog.'

Suddenly, a few yards ahead of the children, Scamper stopped dead and began yapping.

'Scamper's found something!' cried Peter. 'Come on!'

The spaniel was standing on the edge of a very

deep pit, not far from the way down into Deep Dingle.

'Watch out!' George told the others, as they came up. 'It goes a long way down.'

The mouth of the huge pit was half hidden by the grass growing around it. 'Oh, of course – the disused gravel pit!' Colin said. 'I'd quite forgotten it existed. We don't often come this way, of course.'

'I can hardly see the bottom,' said Jack.

'I've got a torch,' said Boris. 'Let's shine it in and see if Brutus is down there.'

The bright beam of his torch lit up the pit – but it was empty apart from some very hard, jagged stones at the bottom.

'Gosh – we were lucky yesterday evening,' said Peter, in a serious tone. 'We must have been quite close to this pit – *I* forgot about it too! If Alice and Colin and I had fallen in, it wouldn't have been very much fun!'

They all shivered, thinking of the bones that might have been broken.

'Still, here we are, safe and sound!' added Peter, more cheerfully.

Just then Scamper, who had gone chasing off again, barked to them from the middle of a coppice of sloe trees. The nine children all ran that way.

'Oh, look!' exclaimed Janet. 'A sort of tunnel going right into the bushes!'

'I'll go along it,' said Alice. And she nimbly made her way into the narrow passage, pushing past the branches. Janet followed her, and then came Pam and Barbara.

The four girls found Scamper in the middle of a tiny clearing at the centre of the bushes.

'This must be where Scamper and Brutus slept last night!' cried Alice. 'The grass is all crushed. Oh, look!' she added excitedly. 'Here's one of Rico's feathers!'

Sure enough, a green feather had caught on a branch, and was quivering in the wind.

The girls emerged from the bushes again – they

didn't need to say what they had found, because the boys had been able to hear all they said as they waited outside.

Scamper was off on the trail of the fugitives again as fast as he could go, with the children after him.

'It's an hour now since we started out!' said Peter, sounding worried. He quickened his pace.

'Yes . . . I just hope we don't arrive too late,' muttered George, glancing meaningfully at him.

They came to the edge of a little wood of fir trees, and the spaniel turned a different way, leaving Deep Dingle behind him and starting back across country towards the village.

The children lost more time because they had to cross ploughed fields. All the rain from the day before made the going heavy, and big lumps of mud stuck to their shoes. They were straggling out in a long line, and to keep it from breaking in two Peter, who was still leading, pulled out the aerial of his walkie-talkie and got in touch with Colin. Colin was bringing up the rear, urging the slower ones on. With the walkie-talkie, he and Peter could keep in contact.

'Hallo, Colin – are you receiving me?'

'Receiving you loud and clear,' said Colin.

'We'll stay in touch all the time now,' said Peter. 'If we get much farther ahead up here, you won't be able to catch up with us . . .'

And just then a irritating, shrill little voice broke into their radio conversation!

'I say, *you* lot got up early, didn't you? This is Susie

74

calling! Ha, ha, ha!'

Jack, who was walking along beside Colin, snatched the walkie-talkie from his friend's hands and shouted at the top of his voice, 'Susie, you little thief! You just shut up! And just you wait – you'd better watch out for those plaits of yours! You'll have short hair by this time tomorrow, I can tell you!'

'OK, I'll shut up,' said Susie, 'but first, perhaps you'd like to know that at this very moment Binkie and I can see Mr Chapman with his dog and his gun!'

'Where is he?' shouted Jack. 'Tell me, or I'll strangle you, Susie!'

'Calm down,' interrupted Peter – of course, *he* had been able to hear this conversation between the brother and sister too. 'Now then, Jack and Susie, don't say anything unless I ask you a question! Get it?' he added threateningly. Then he went on more calmly, 'Right, Susie – where exactly *are* you and Binkie?'

'Oh, we're at the crossroads,' said the little pest Susie, in an offhand way.

Peter, George and Boris were standing in the middle of the field, and Peter ran to the end of it. From there, he looked to his left, and he could see the figures of Susie and Binkie standing out against the grey sky. Now and then the aerial of the walkie-talkie they had with them caught the light, and he could see it glinting. The two girls were at the foot of a cross on a stone pedestal where two roads met.

'Hallo, Susie,' he said. 'Yes, I can see you both now – can *you* see *me*?'

'You bet I can,' she said. 'I can see George and Boris coming up behind you too.'

Peter turned round, and sure enough, the other two had almost reached him.

'But I don't see any sign of Mr Chapman,' he said. 'You were bluffing just now, weren't you?'

'No, we weren't!' said Susie, annoyed because he didn't believe her. 'I can see him from here as well as I can see you!'

'Where is he?' asked Peter.

'I'll tell you, but only on one condition. You must let Binkie and me be in the Secret Seven!'

'Well, we won't!' said Jack indignantly.

'I said you weren't to interrupt unless I asked you a question!' Peter said firmly. Trying to keep calm, he went on talking to Susie.

'Now listen to me, Susie and Binkie! If Mr Chapman finds Brutus before we do, he'll probably ill him, and it will be your fault!'

'Well then, will you let us join the Secret Seven? Yes or no?' Susie insisted. 'If you say no, then it'll be our fault if your precious Brutus gets killed, Peter!'

Alice, who had heard the end of this conversation, came running up to Peter. 'Oh, please do as they say!' she begged. 'Please, please do!'

Peter realized he just had to give in. He was about to reply when he heard Jack's voice over the walkie-talkie.

'Peter – I've spotted Mr Chapman! He's about a hundred yards to your right, at the foot of a big oak tree!'

'Where?' cried Peter, looking round.

'On the edge of a beet field! Look – there, where a blackbird has just flown up!'

'I can see the blackbird, but not Mr Chapman. Wait a minute, we'll move somewhere else.'

Along wth George, Boris and Alice, Peter ran to the other end of the field – and sure enough, now he could see the chemist and his dog not far from an oak tree. Mr Chapman was walking briskly towards a field of maize. The maize had been harvested, but the plants were still standing.

'I've spotted him!' he shouted down the walkie talkie. 'Thanks, Jack! Now —'

'Rhubarb-rhubarb-rhubarb-rhubarb!' shouted terrible Susie, and she went on shouting it. She wanted to muddle up the air waves and stop the Secret Seven talking to each other.

'That little pest is getting her revenge!' said George angrily.

'Let's just cut her off!' said Peter, breaking radio contact.

'But where's Scamper gone?' asked Boris.

'Yes – where *has* he gone this time?' asked Peter in surprise.

'I saw him making for the maize fields too,' said Alice.

And at that moment the spaniel emerged from the field of tall plants, wagging his tail as if to say, 'What are you all waiting for? Why don't you come with me?'

'Let's go!' said Peter. 'But I think we'll skirt round the edge of the field – I don't much want to get into Mr Chapman's line of fire!'

As the four children were making for Scamper, Pam joined them. She was out of breath.

'We couldn't catch what you were saying when Susie started chattering away like that,' she gasped, 'but I've come to tell you Colin and the others are making for the maize field too – from the other side.'

'Good!' said Peter. 'So the field will be surrounded! Brutus won't escape us this time!'

'And nor will Mr Chapman,' added George.

Peter gave them the signal to set off, and they advanced cautiously, trying not to attract Mr Chapman's attention. And at the same moment Jack was leaving Colin's party, and creeping cautiously towards the crossroads! Twenty yards from the cross, he hid in some tall grass on a patch of waste land. He could hear his little sister, quite clearly, as she chanted away all sorts of nonsense.

'Silly Secret Seven, yah, yah, yah! Rhubarb-rhubarb-rhubarb! Silly old stupid old soppy Secret Seven!' She was still jamming their air waves!

Jack just couldn't bear it any longer. He jumped up and ran towards the two little pests! Taken by surprise, Susie and Binkie dropped the walkie-talkie and made their escape. Watching them run away, Jack couldn't help smiling. He knew if he went after them he'd easily win the race, but he wanted to scare them just a little more, so he wasn't going to catch them straight away! Playing cat and mouse with them, he let them run on ahead of him, squawking in alarm – and then he put on a spurt of his own! He wanted his revenge! In a moment he had caught up with them, and he took them by the scruff of the neck, one with each hand. Terrified, the two girls stood perfectly still.

'Now then!' he said sternly, letting go of Binkie. 'You just clear out, Binkie, or I'll murder you!'

Binkie was so scared she didn't move – so Jack made a threatening gesture, and then she began to run, letting out shrill little cries! Next Jack turned to his sister Susie, still holding her firmly.

'So it's just the two of us!' he said, grinning! 'And we have a score to settle! You're going to tell me how you found out about our expedition this morning, *and* how you managed to steal my walkie-talkie!'

Susie tried to wriggle free, but Jack held on, and she had to explain. 'Yesterday evening I saw Pam talking to Alice in the road. I guessed something was up – so I followed Alice, and after you let her into the shed I only had to listen at the keyhole.'

'And what about the walkie-talkie?' shouted Jack, shaking her.

'Well, you *know* what a heavy sleeper you are, Jack!' said Susie, in a sarcastic voice. 'Lying there snoring . . .'

'Never mind that!' yelled Jack.

'So I got into your bedroom just after you went to sleep last night,' Susie went on, 'and then it was easy to find where you'd hidden the walkie-talkie. In that big old jar! You'd better think of somewhere more secret another time if you — '

But she didn't say any more, because Jack, furious, had grabbed her two thick pigtails and was tying

them into knots. The little girl yelled, and Jack shouted even louder. 'This'll keep you going while you wait for me and my scissors! Now clear out, and stay out of my sight!'

Susie was only too glad to obey! She hurried off to join Binkie, who was waiting for her at a distance, hidden behind a tree.

Jack felt better! He hoped those two pests would have learnt their lesson, and the Secret Seven would be rid of them and their tormenting ways for good! He turned round and went over to the crossroads, to pick up the walkie-talkie which his sister had dropped there.

Chapter Nine

BRUTUS IS BACK

At that moment Peter and his party reached the edge of the maize field.

'Colin must be in position on the other side by now,' said Peter in a low voice, 'so we'll spread out all round the field.'

But then they heard a sound – the noise of leaves and stems being trampled and crushed broke the silence!

'That noise is somewhere in the middle of the field!' whispered George.

Of course, the plants were too tall for them to be able to see what was going on.

'It's Brutus!' whispered Alice.

'Come on!' Boris told his sister.

'Be careful!' Peter told them.

Alice was clutching the lion's muzzle and chain as if it would bring her luck. With her brother, she made her way into the thick forest of maize plants. The two young circus folk disappeared from sight.

Peter, George and Pam felt a lump in their throats as they watched Alice and Boris go. Would everything be all right? Was Brutus really as harmless as Alice said?

Suddenly they jumped – as they heard Jack's cheerful voice over the radio!

'Hey, Peter – I've got the walkie-talkie back! And I've sent Susie off with a flea in her ear!'

Then, suddenly, the tone of his voice changed as he said in alarm, 'Oh, watch out – do be careful! Mr Chapman's just gone into the maize field with his gun raised ready to shoot!'

'Oh no!' cried Pam in horror. 'He may hit Alice and Boris!'

'We mustn't panic,' said Peter, though he too was alarmed. 'Colin's on the other side of the field, with Janet and Barbara – they could create a diversion. Hallo, Colin – Colin? Can you hear me?' he called tensely.

And then – four shots rang out!

The sound was followed by echoes, and a great deal of squealing. Automatically, Peter, George and Pam had flung themselves flat on the ground. When they raised their heads they couldn't make out what was going on! What *was* that squealing noise? And there was a low thudding sound too, a little like horse's hoofs. Then they heard the piercing cry of Rico the parrot up in the air above them. And then . . .

'Got him!' exclaimed a man's voice triumphantly. 'Got him!'

The three children leaped to their feet.

'That was Mr Chapman!' cried Peter.

'Oh, he's killed poor Brutus!' sobbed Pam.

'Watch out — look, over there!' yelled George, pointing to the edge of the field. The plants were waving about as if a storm of wind was blowing through them! Then there was a tremendous crashing noise as the stalks were broken and trodden down by whatever was moving about there. The three children stayed just where they were — they simply didn't understand what was happening.

And then, only three or four yards away from them, about ten large, pink creatures shot out of the maize field and galloped past at top speed!

'My word — pigs!' cried Peter at the top of his voice.

Pam opened her mouth, but she couldn't utter a sound. George was rooted to the spot, goggling at the animals!

The pigs went on past the children without even noticing them. They were well away by the time Peter heard Colin's voice on his walkie-talkie.

'Hallo, Peter — Colin calling! It's all right! Boris has just got Brutus's muzzle safely on him, and they're coming back through the field your way!'

George and Pam heaved a sigh of relief at this news.

'Then — what did Mr Chapman shoot?' asked Peter.

'Oh, he made a splendid kill!' said Colin. 'I saw it! He brought down a very large pig! I think the pigs

must belong to Farmer Brown – this is his land, and I expect the pigs got out of the farmyard and hid in the maize plants! Oh, won't Farmer Brown be cross! I expect Mr Chapman will have to pay him compensation!'

Peter burst out laughing! It had been a close shave,

but everything had turned out all right in the end, thank goodness.

Soon Boris and Alice came out of the field, along with Brutus. They were smiling broadly, and as for the lion, he didn't seem at all bothered by all the activity around him. He was picking his way through the plants like a huge cat, with Rico perched on his back.

Scamper ran to Peter and rolled at his feet to be patted, wagging his tail harder than ever.

'Well done, Scamper! Good dog – you did splendidly!'

A few moments later Colin arrived, with Janet and Barbara. Pam told them how alarming it had been when the pigs dashed out of the field. 'There must have been nearly a dozen of them!' she said excitedly.

'But what started them stampeding through the field like that?' asked George.

'I think I may be responsible,' said Colin, smiling. You see, *we* heard some noise too, over at the other side of the field. We thought of Brutus, straight away. So I went into the field, leaving Barbara and Janet at the edge of it – and as I made my way through the maize I bumped into the pigs, and they started dashing about in confusion!'

Everyone burst out laughing! Trying to keep a straight face, Colin went on, 'And the biggest pig of all jolly nearly knocked Mr Chapman down – it blundered right past his legs!'

'I suppose he could hardly miss, if it was so close!' said Peter, chuckling.

Just then Jack came running up to join the others. *He* was all excited too. 'You'll never guess what I've just seen!' he cried. 'About a dozen big pink pigs on the loose!'

'Don't be silly. You must be joking!' said George, straight-faced.

'But I tell you, I did see them. There were at least ten, maybe more,' Jack said earnestly.

Unable to control themselves any longer, the other eight broke into gales of laughter again, and told him all about the comical end of their adventure.

It wasn't even eight o'clock by the time the Seven and their friends from the Jungle Circus arrived back in the village. They had heard the police announcement, of course, but they were still quite surprised to find the place utterly deserted. There was nobody and nothing to be seen – not so much as a cat or a dog about!

With Brutus at the head of the procession, they walked through the silent streets.

'Gosh!' said Pam. 'It's creepy – like one of those old war films!'

'It's not a bit creepy!' Jack told her. 'We've found Brutus, and everything's all right!'

'Hooray!' cried Barbara and Janet in chorus, and they struck up a merry song. Soon they were all singing at the tops of their voices. Even Scamper was barking in time to the tune!

In a few minutes windows began to open, and you could see the village coming back to life. People came out into the street to congratulate the children. By the time they reached the circus field there was quite a long procession of admiring villagers following them. To the sound of loud cheers, Peter and his friends went up to a Land-Rover where the inspector and Mr Kriloff were sitting.

'Mission accomplished!' said Peter, proudly.

'Well done, children!' said Mr Kriloff, hugging Alice and Boris, and shaking hands warmly with the Seven.

'Yes, very well done,' said the inspector. 'Well, now I can call off the hunt, and tell my men to come back into the village.'

'Were they really out searching? We never saw any of them,' said Peter.

'I'm not surprised,' said the inspector. 'You see, I sent them out at five this morning to take up positions all round the village in a huge circle about seven miles in radius. Their orders were to close in on the village, searching the countryside as they went. But you moved faster than they did!'

'It was all due to Scamper,' said Peter, picking up the spaniel.

'I don't quite understand,' Colin told the inspector. 'You say the policemen were all starting their search seven miles away? But we heard the coaches arriving about five-thirty this morning.

'That's right,' said the inspector. 'They were empty, though – coming here ready to pick the men up again once the circle was closed!'

Now everything was clear! Alice, Boris and the Seven took Brutus back to his cage, as the crowd looked on, clapping and cheering.

Just in case, Mr Kriloff had been careful to put Tutti-Frutti the little monkey in a cage well away from Brutus!

And as for Susie and Binkie, they were watching the happy scene as they hid behind the caravan – and quivering with rage!

There were so many people who wanted to see the show that afternoon that the little Jungle Circus had to turn some away. And the performance itself was a huge success, especially Boris's brilliant lion-taming act.

But the Secret Seven agreed that the acting honours really went to Brutus, the gentle lion, who put on a marvellous performance as a fierce, savage wild beast!

If you have enjoyed this book, you may like to read some more exciting adventures from Knight Books:

A complete list of new adventures about the SECRET SEVEN

KNIGHT BOOKS

A complete list of the SECRET SEVEN ADVENTURES by Enid Blyton

KNIGHT BOOKS

A complete list of the FAMOUS FIVE ADVENTURES by Enid Blyton

1. FIVE ON A TREASURE ISLAND
2. FIVE GO ADVENTURING AGAIN
3. FIVE RUN AWAY TOGETHER
4. FIVE GO TO SMUGGLER'S TOP
5. FIVE GO OFF IN A CARAVAN
6. FIVE ON KIRRIN ISLAND AGAIN
7. FIVE GO OFF TO CAMP
8. FIVE GET INTO TROUBLE
9. FIVE FALL INTO ADVENTURE
10. FIVE ON A HIKE TOGETHER
11. FIVE HAVE A WONDERFUL TIME
12. FIVE GO DOWN TO THE SEA
13. FIVE GO TO MYSTERY MOOR
14. FIVE HAVE PLENTY OF FUN
15. FIVE ON A SECRET TRAIL
16. FIVE GO TO BILLYCOCK HILL
17. FIVE GET INTO A FIX
18. FIVE ON FINNISTON FARM
19. FIVE GO TO DEMON'S ROCKS
20. FIVE HAVE A MYSTERY TO SOLVE
21. FIVE ARE TOGETHER AGAIN

KNIGHT BOOKS

A complete list of new adventures about the FAMOUS FIVE

KNIGHT BOOKS